There's a

in the Library!

ORCHARD BOOKS

First published in Great Britain in 2020
by The Watts Publishing Group

10 9 8 7 6 5 4 3 2 1

Text © Dave Skinner, 2020
Illustrations © Aurélie Guillerey, 2020

The moral rights of the author and
illustrator have been asserted.

A CIP catalogue record for this book is
available from the British Library.

HB ISBN 978 1 40835 351 6
PB ISBN 978 1 40835 352 3

Printed and bound in China

MIX
Paper from
responsible sources
FSC® C104740
www.fsc.org

Orchard Books
An imprint of Hachette Children's Group
Part of The Watts Publishing Group Limited

Carmelite House
50 Victoria Embankment
London EC4Y 0DZ

An Hachette UK Company
www.hachette.co.uk

www.hachettechildrens.co.uk

With love to Sally-Anne,
Charlie and Grace.
And with thanks to Emily,
for keeping the faith!
D.S.

For Ambroise
and Clovis
A.G.

Dave Skinner

Aurélie Guillerey

There's a

LiON

in the

Library!

ORCHARD

This is little Lucy Lupin.

With her **darling** dimples,
her **charming** freckles
and her **adorable** button nose,
little Lucy Lupin looks like the **sweetest**,
nicest, **loveliest** little girl in all the world.

But she isn't.

These are some of little Lucy Lupin's favourite things to do …

But of **all** the terrible things little Lucy Lupin loves to do, her FAVOURITE is telling big fat lies.

One Monday morning, little Lucy Lupin walked into the library
and said to the librarian:

"THERE'S A LION
IN THE LIBRARY!
I saw him in the History section,
chewing on a book about the
Ancient Egyptians.
Maybe he escaped
from the zoo?"

The librarian took a good long look at little Lucy Lupin —
at her darling dimples, and her charming freckles,
and her adorable button nose ...

... and then she climbed onto her chair and shouted,

"Everybody out!
This is an emergency!
Please leave the library AT ONCE!"

Soon little Lucy Lupin found herself outside the library with all the people who'd wanted to be inside the library, while police officers and firemen and vets with nets searched the building.

"Little girl, are you SURE you saw a lion?" asked the Chief Fire Officer.

Little Lucy Lupin
nodded her head.

"Well, we can't find him," said the Chief Fire Officer.
"That naughty old lion must have snuck out the back door."

And little Lucy Lupin laughed all the way home.

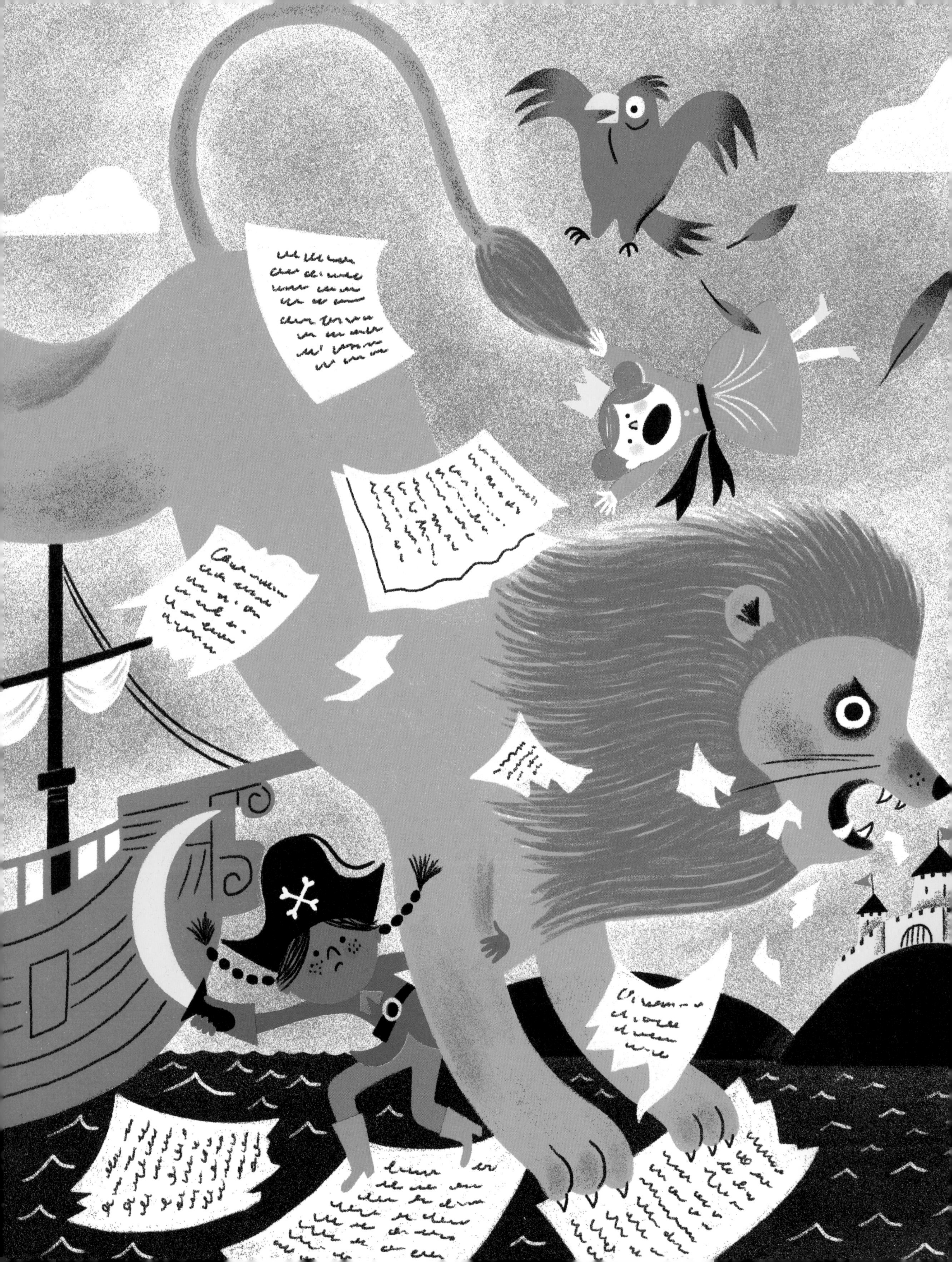

The next day, little Lucy Lupin went back to the library and said to the caretaker:

"THERE'S A LION IN THE LIBRARY! I saw him in the Romance section, tearing up a book about a princess and a pirate. Maybe he escaped from the circus?"

The caretaker took a good long look at little Lucy Lupin — at her dimples, and her freckles and her button nose ...

… and then he pressed an alarm button and shouted,

**"The library is closing!
Everybody out, NOW!"**

The police officers and firemen and vets with nets searched the building.

But they found no lion.

And little Lucy Lupin
laughed all the way home.

On the third day, little Lucy Lupin skipped into
the library and said to the coffee shop manager:

"THERE'S A LION IN THE LIBRARY!
I saw him in the Geography section, licking a book about oceans.
Maybe he escaped from a ship?"

The coffee shop manager took a good long look at little Lucy Lupin —
at her dimples, freckles and button nose …

… and then he threw away the muffin he'd been eating and yelled,

"There's a **lion** in the library! RUN FOR YOUR LIVES!"

And so, for the third time, little Lucy Lupin waited
outside the library, while police officers and
firemen and vets with nets searched the building.

But they found no lion.
And on the way home,
little Lucy Lupin
laughed so hard
she nearly made herself sick.

That night, the librarian, the caretaker and the coffee shop manager
got together to talk about the mystery of the lion in the library.

"At first I didn't
believe her," said
the caretaker …

"But then I took a good long look at those darling dimples, and charming freckles, and adorable button nose, and I thought, this little girl looks so sweet and nice and lovely, she must be telling the truth."

"Me too!" said the others.

"Hmm," said the librarian, "you know, when I was a little girl, I was sweet and nice and lovely too. In fact, I was SO sweet and nice, I could get away with just about ANYTHING."

And, one by one, they began to wonder …

A few days later, little Lucy Lupin was in the library again when in through an open window jumped a real, live, genuine lion – with a big bushy mane, long shiny claws, and sharp white teeth.

"THERE'S A LION IN THE LIBRARY!"

shouted little Lucy Lupin.

"A lion? I doubt that very much," said the caretaker.

"Ha, I don't **think** so," said the coffee shop manager.

"I suppose he's **chasing** you around the library,
swishing his tail and licking his lips?" said the librarian.

"YES!" cried little Lucy Lupin.
"That's **just** what he's doing!"

"You are a **very naughty girl** for telling such lies!" said the librarian.

And she went back to stacking her books.

And the caretaker went back to mopping his floor.

And the coffee shop manager went back to eating his muffin.

And none of them thought any more about little Lucy Lupin.

Until **suddenly** they heard what sounded **very** much like the …

ROAR of a lion.

But by then, it was too late.

And you know what?
Little Lucy Lupin wasn't sweet, or nice, or lovely ...

... but she was DELICIOUS.